BEARS DON'T CRY!

Emma Chichester Clark

HarperCollins *Children's Books*

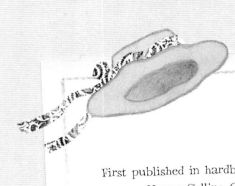

First published in hardback in the United Kingdom by
HarperCollins *Children's Books* in 2022

1 3 5 7 9 10 8 6 4 2

ISBN: 978-0-00-849183-3

HarperCollins *Children's Books* is a division of
HarperCollins *Publishers* Ltd,
1 London Bridge Street, London SE1 9GF

Visit our website at: www.harpercollins.co.uk

Printed in China

THIS BOOK BELONGS TO

_____

_____

George was no ordinary bear.
He lived in the summerhouse in a garden
belonging to his dear friend Clementine,
and her mother. Clementine had
taught George to read.

Clementine and her mother **loved** George.

He was very good company and
always helpful around the house.

He was never happier

than when
he felt . . .

. . . he was being useful.

Each day, when Clementine went to school
and her mother went to work, George would
settle down in the back garden to read.

Clementine's mother left him with **wonderful**
books she'd got from the library.

One day, George finished his book early. He knew it would be a long time before Clementine and her mother came home, so he decided to be very brave and go to the library all by himself.

'Why have I never done this before?' he wondered, as he strolled along the sunny street.

Well, it really was a lovely sunny day. But the sight of
a large, wild, brown bear ambling along the road
had sparked a panic all over town. So when George
arrived at the library, he found that it was closed.

'Bother!' said George.

On the other side of the street there was a shop selling newspapers.

'They'll know what time the library opens,' thought George.

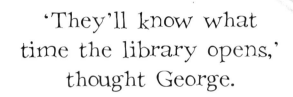

But suddenly, and mysteriously, the newspaper shop was closed too.

'**Bother!**' said George. 'Just missed it.'

Next, George went to the cake shop to ask about the library, but it said CLOSED on the door.

'I'm sure it was open a moment ago,' sighed George.
'Things happen quickly here,' he thought.
'I suppose that's what towns are like.'

The market was buzzing with people, so George headed over there.

'If only **someone** would stop for a second.'

But before he had even said 'Hello' or 'Excuse me', everyone had vanished.

The market was empty . . .

or was it?

George bent down to look.

'AIEEE!'

'HELP!'

Shrieked the stallholders.

George leapt back in alarm. 'OH!' he cried.

'Oh, no . . .' cried George.

'I can't stop . . .

SAVE ME!' cried George.

'H-E-L-P!'

And there was something no one
had expected to see!

A flying bear . . .

a galumphing, great bear, flying across the square.

The crowd gaped and gasped. And then . . .

they laughed.

Mamma mia!

Oh! My heavenly days!
Now, I've seen
everything!

Oh, poor George!
Everything had happened so quickly.

What a disaster . . .

But why was everyone laughing? He wondered. They weren't laughing at **him** . . . were they?

And the library book . . . George fished it out
of the water. It was **ruined,** of course.

'How clumsy I am,' he sighed.
'How hopeless and clumsy.'

He climbed out of
the pool sadly. But just
then, Clementine ran
out from the crowd.

When George saw her,
he **burst** into tears.

The crowd went quiet.
Then somebody whispered,

'Bears don't cry, do they?'

Clementine looked at poor George and then she looked at the crowd. Then she stood up and spoke to them.

'This is my dear friend, George,' she said.
'He may be big – but you have hurt his feelings.'

Everyone looked at each other. They
didn't think a big bear would cry. But
that's exactly what had happened.

Somebody came forward
and gave George a towel, and someone
else gave him a hankie, and then
everyone went to say sorry to him.

They were all
really, truly sorry.

The librarian brought George a new library book.
She said, 'Don't worry about the old one.
I'll take it home and dry it out.'

And then someone in the crowd said
'Bears don't **read**, do they?'

So, George stood up, nervously.
He opened the book and began reading.

And that was another thing no one
had expected to see – but it was a
wonderful thing, and they all stood
quietly, listening to George until
the book was finished.

The next day, the
librarian came to tea
with Clementine and her
mother and George.

There was just one anxious moment . . .

. . . when everyone held
their breath . . .

. . . and feared disaster . . .

. . . but it all
turned out perfectly,
in the end.